W9-BUC-904

For those who place just the right book
at just the right time in the hands of a young reader —M.C.

To my brother Matt, whose passion for
knowledge (and right hook) are legendary —A.H.

Text copyright © 2011 by Mary Casanova
Pictures copyright © 2011 by Ard Hoyt
All rights reserved
Distributed in Canada by D&M Publishers, Inc.
Color separations by Chroma Graphics
Printed in August 2011 in China by South China Printing Co. Ltd.,
Dongguan City, Guangdong Province
Designed by Jay Colvin
First edition, 2011
3   5   7   9   10   8   6   4   2

www.fsgkidsbooks.com

Library of Congress Cataloging-in-Publication Data
Casanova, Mary.
    The day Dirk Yeller came to town / Mary Casanova ; pictures by Ard Hoyt.— 1st ed.
        p.   cm.
    Summary: When outlaw Dirk Yeller arrives in town looking for something to take
away his cat-scratch fever, young Sam, whose pa says he is "a world-a-trouble and curious
as a tomcat," knows just what this dangerous and jittery criminal needs to calm him down.
    ISBN: 978-0-374-31742-3
    [1. Robbers and outlaws—Fiction.   2. Libraries—Fiction.   3. Books and reading—Fiction.
4. West (U.S.)—Fiction.]   I. Hoyt, Ard, ill.   II. Title.
PZ7.C266Day 2011
[E]—dc22
                                                                                    2009024671

Mary Casanova   **Pictures by Ard Hoyt**

THE DAY DIRK YELLER CAME TO TOWN

Farrar Straus Giroux
New York

The day Dirk Yeller came to town, the wind curled its lip, cattle quit lowin', and tumbleweeds stopped tumblin' along.

R0433317749

Townsfolk whispered. "He starts stampedes!"
"He holds up trains!"
"He's trouble!"

But I reckoned Dirk Yeller had come at a good time, 'cuz I'd just hit a home run through a window. Pa always said, "Sam, you're a world-o'-trouble and curious as a tomcat." So when Dirk Yeller tromped into the post office, I dropped my broom to follow.

"I'm lookin' for somethin'," the outlaw growled, "to take away my cat scratch fever!" His fingers were a-itchin' and a-twitchin'.

The postmaster backed away.
But I wasn't worried. Sometimes I was fidgety, too.
The postmaster stammered, "T-t-try some Calming Elixir from the general store!"

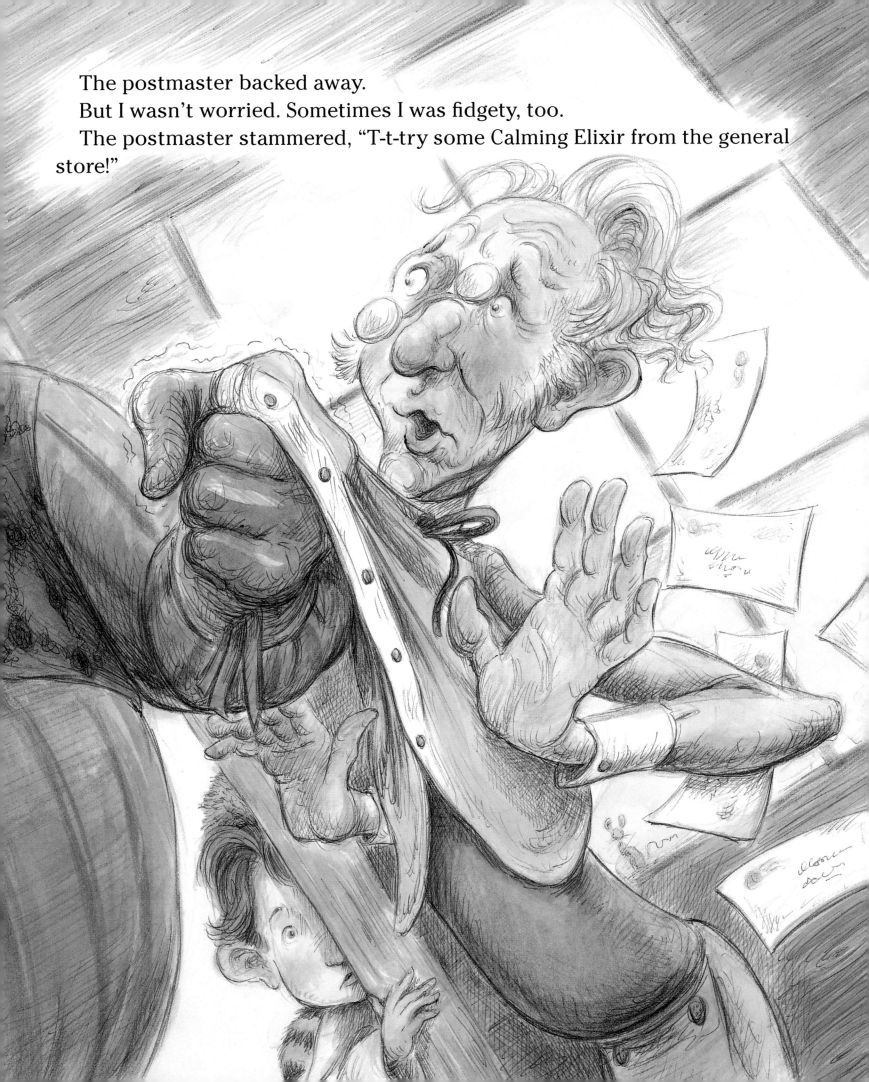

At the general store, merchandise went a-flyin'. "I'm lookin' for somethin'," Dirk Yeller said, "to keep a coyote from bayin' at the moon!"

Mrs. Peterson drew her children close. "Have mercy!"

But I wasn't scared. Sometimes I felt a little wild, too. Why, just yesterday I'd dropped a toad down the back of Emma Peterson's dress.

Mrs. Peterson trembled. "Try those live traps over at the trading post!"

I skedaddled, too.

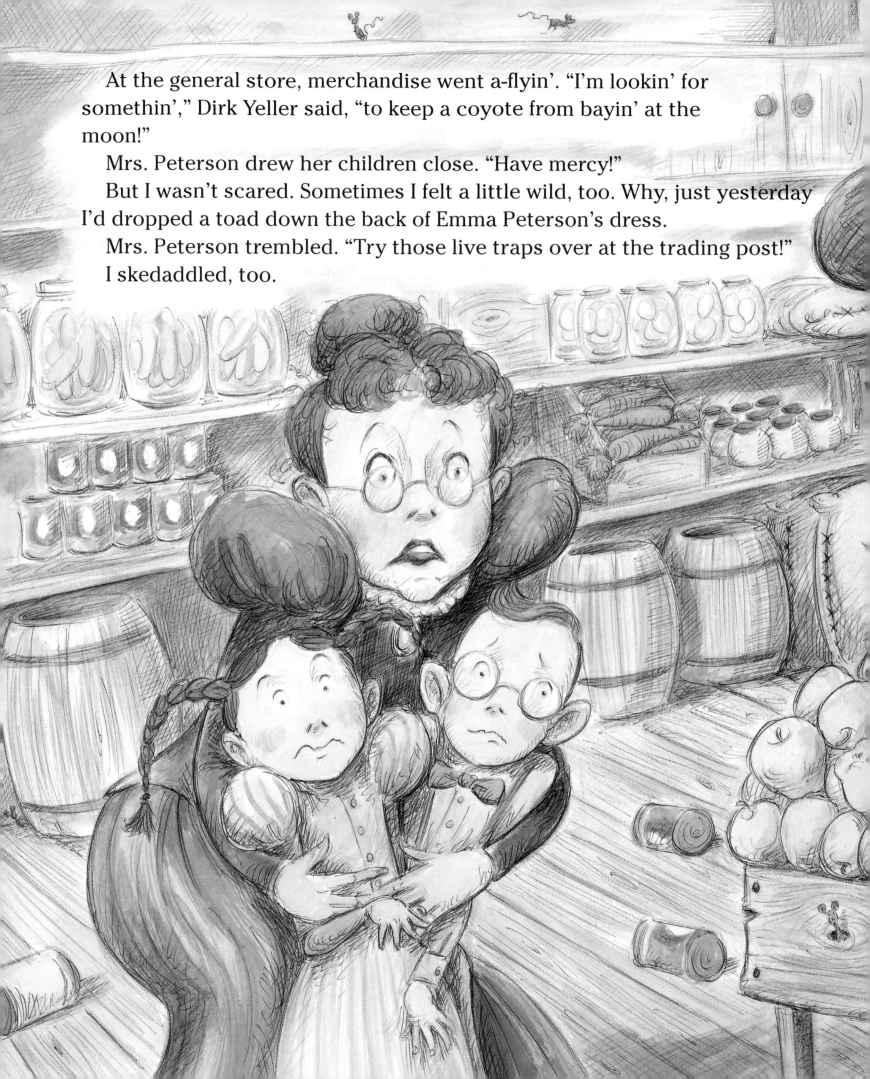

At the trading post, rakes and shovels clattered.

"I'm fixin' to find somethin'," said Dirk, "to keep jumping beans from jumpin'!"

Like Dirk Yeller, sometimes I was jumpy, too.

Shorty wiped his brow. "I know nothin' about jumping beans, but maybe you'd like some new boots."

Dirk Yeller shook his head.

"Well, go try the saloon!"

At the saloon, Dirk's fingers were a-itchin'
and a-twitchin'. His eyes were train-tunnel dark.
"Must be somethin' here," he boomed, "to keep
rattlesnakes from rattlin'!"
Customers darted for safety.

But clear as well water, Dirk Yeller just couldn't sit still.
"What you need," said Swaggerin' Sal, "is a nice cup of hot coffee. Try the jailhouse!"
Dirk Yeller stomped out.

At the jailhouse, Dirk Yeller warned, "I'm itchin' for somethin', and I won't stop until I find what I'm lookin' for!"

"We're peace-lovin' folk," said the sheriff, "and I'm servin' you notice. Ride your horse outta town before sundown!"

Dirk Yeller gulped the sheriff's coffee, then left with a slam.

The sheriff spotted me. "Sam?"

I tipped my hat and scrammed.

Down the boardwalk, Dirk Yeller stomped.
Through dust and dung, Dirk Yeller clomped.
And in the middle of the street—he stopped.

I suddenly remembered what always helped me. I gulped down my jitters and stepped into the outlaw's shadow.

Dirk Yeller's eyes drilled into my backbone. But I held my ground and stood tall, like a world-o'-trouble. "Dirk Yeller," I said, "if I can show you how to stop your itchin' and twitchin' and your jumpin' and rattlin'—will you promise to leave our town in peace?"

The outlaw gave a snort, which I took to mean yes.
"Then follow me!"

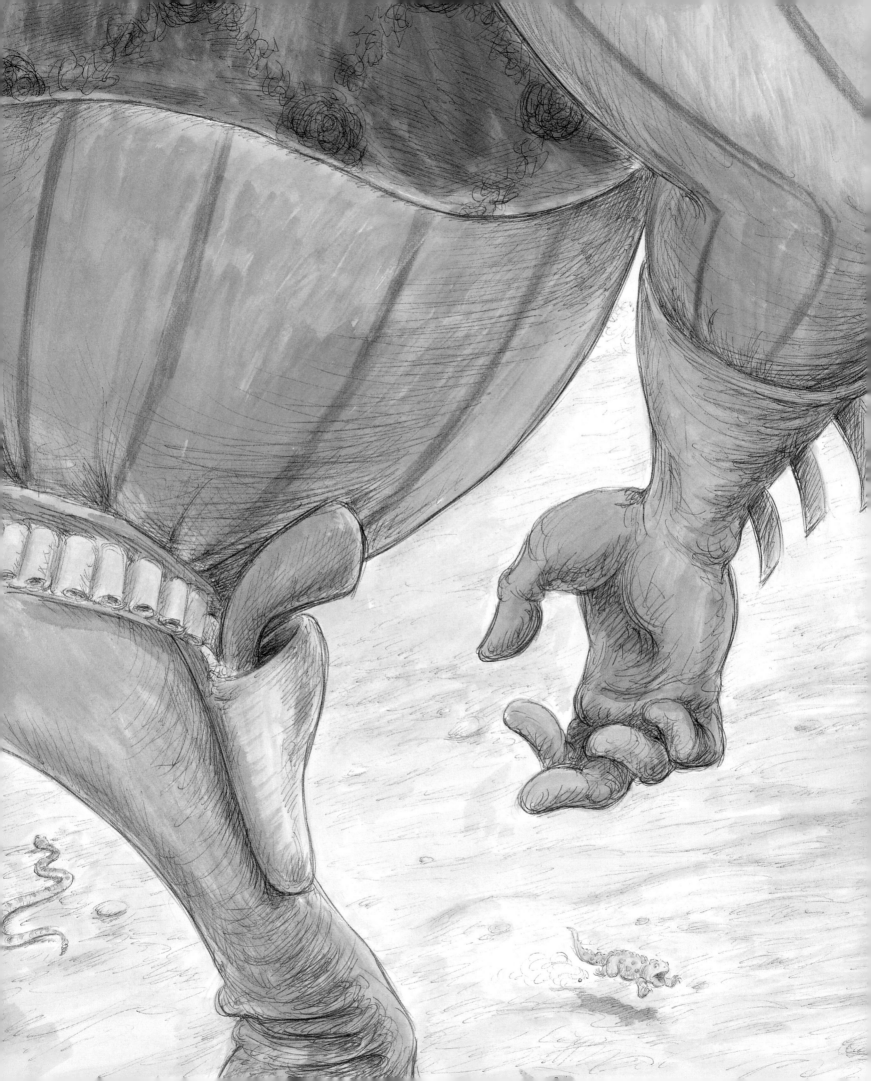

To my relief—glory be!—Dirk Yeller tromped right after me.

Inside the new building, he was itchin' like a dog scratchin' fleas. His eyes were coiled for trouble.

But Miss Jenny didn't seem scared. Sweet as pecan pie, she asked, "May I help you?"

"I'm lookin' for somethin'," Dirk Yeller grumbled, "to take away my cat scratch fever, to keep coyotes from bayin' at the moon, to keep jumping beans from jumpin', to keep rattlesnakes from—"

"Come with me."

Then she led the way to a tall stack of books. "This one," she asked, "or perhaps this?"

Dirk Yeller opened a book, then started to mouth the words. I could tell he wasn't a real strong reader. When he stumbled on a hard word, his face turned red as Ma's blue-ribbon tomatoes.

So I whispered, "Here, Mr. Yeller, let me help."

Together, we sounded out word after word.

Soon, Dirk Yeller was turning one page, then another.

And the more the outlaw read, the less he itched and twitched. The more he read, the less he jumped and jittered. Sure as shootin', Dirk Yeller was sitting *still*.

Before long, the sun sank low.
The sheriff rattled handcuffs in warning.
And then Miss Jenny called out, "Closing time!"
The outlaw glared. "I'll . . . be . . . back."
The townsfolk froze. And I froze, too. What if I'd been all wrong?

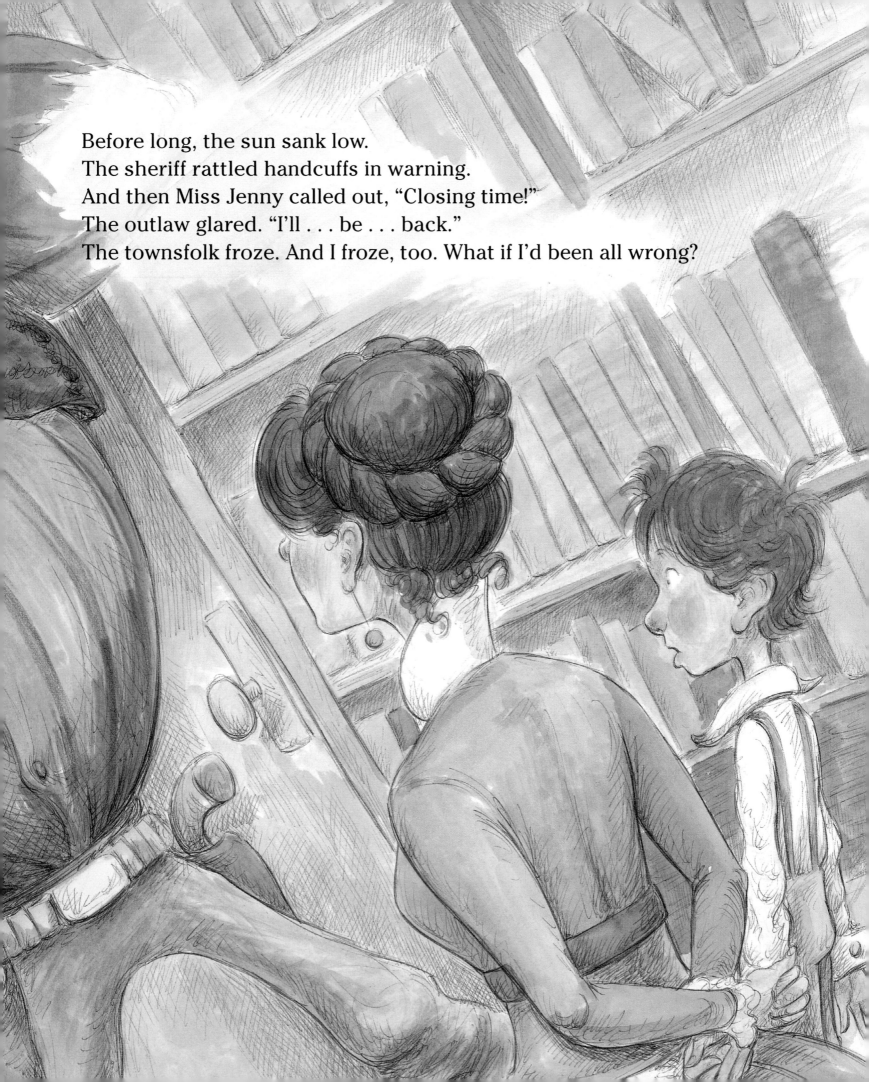

"I'll be back," Dirk Yeller said, "to check out more books!"
The people cheered.

And then he winked. "And to see Miss Jenny."

Saddlebags full, Dirk Yeller rode off into the sunset.
The wind blew a sigh of relief, cattle started lowin',
and tumbleweeds went back to tumblin' along.

And ever since, the library has become the busiest place in town,
especially for folks with curious, restless minds—

like Dirk Yeller and me.